DOCTOR·WHO

3 1336 10084 1197

THE DOCTOR

BBC CHILDREN'S BOOKS
Published by the Penguin Group
Penguin Books Ltd, 80 Strand, London, WC2R 0RL, England
Penguin Group (USA), Inc., 375 Hudson Street, New York, New York 10014, USA
Penguin Books (Australia) Ltd, 250 Camberwell Road, Camberwell, Victoria 3124, Australia.
(A division of Pearson Australia Group Pty Ltd)
Canada, India, New Zealand, South Africa.
Published by BBC Children's Books, 2006
Text and design © Children's Character Books, 2006
Images © BBC 2004
Written by Jacqueline Rayner. The Hero Factor by Stephen Cole.
10 9 8 7 6
Printed in China.
ISBN-13: 978-1-40590-245-8

CONTENTS

There's no one in the universe quite like the Doctor. At first glance he looks like a human, but he's really a Time Lord, one of a race of very powerful beings. In fact, he's the last of the Time Lords — the only one of his people to survive the horrific Time War against the Daleks.

But even before the destruction of his people, the Doctor was unique. Instead of staying at home, he chose to 'borrow' a time machine and explore the universe. Instead of just observing other planets, he chose to get involved in their affairs. And instead of following the easy path, he chose to stand up for what is right. Whatever the cost.

Luckily for us, Earth is the Doctor's favourite planet. He sometimes despairs of the human race, but he will always be there to defend them from harm. The Doctor may have had ten bodies and travelled with dozens of different companions, but one thing doesn't change, he'll always be a hero.

Name: No one knows! He's always called just 'the Doctor'

Age: approx. 900 years old

Height: 1.85m (6'1")

Hair: Brown

Eyes: Brown

Home planet: Gallifrey, now destroyed

Current home: The TARDIS

Species: Time Lord

Profession: Adventurer

DOCTOR ANATOMY

Trendy sideburns

1.85m tall (6'1")

Glasses for examining things closely

Mole between his shoulder blades

New 'fighting' hand, grown to replace the one cut off by the Sycorax Leader

Ever-useful sonic screwdriver

Respiratory bypass system allows the Doctor to go without oxygen for a short time

Suit lets him blend in on present-day Earth

Comfy plimsolls

TEST YOUR KNOWLEDGE

ROSE

The Doctor wasn't looking for a companion when he came to Earth to foil the invasion plans of the Nestene Consciousness, but he seemed fated to meet human teenager Rose Tyler. First he saved her from the deadly Autons, then tracked an Auton arm to her flat, and then rescued her from the attack of a Nestene-created duplicate. They ended up confronting the Consciousness together and it was Rose's turn to save the Doctor's life. It soon became clear that the Time Lord and the ordinary human girl belonged together. Rose later went to extraordinary lengths to save the Doctor's life again, when she absorbed the whole of the Time Vortex and defeated the Daleks.

SARAH JANE

Journalist Sarah Jane Smith first met the third Doctor when she was working undercover to get a story. To start with, she thought the Doctor was a baddie! But they soon became firm friends and Sarah and the Doctor had many exciting adventures together. Until the Doctor left Sarah on Earth when he was summoned to his home planet, and never came back for her. Sarah was stunned to meet the tenth Doctor many years later, when she was once more investigating a story, and was soon caught up in the fight against the Krillitanes. Although the Doctor invited Sarah to travel with him again, she decided that her place was on Earth, but no matter what, Sarah will always occupy a very special place in the Doctor's hearts.

K-9

K-9 — the Doctor's 'second best friend' — is a mobile computer in the shape of a dog. He originally came from the year 5000, having been built by a scientist called Professor Marius who was missing his pet. The Doctor travelled with two different K-9s before building a third to send to his friend, Sarah Jane Smith, on Earth. K-9 is as loyal as a real dog, and will defend his master, the Doctor, and his mistress, Sarah Jane, to the end. But he has several things that a real dog doesn't have, like a blaster in his nose, a tail antenna and extensive databanks. K-9 sacrificed himself to defeat the Krillitanes, but the Doctor once again replaced him with a new and improved model.

MICKEY

The Doctor offered Mickey the chance to travel in the TARDIS soon after they met, but scared Mickey turned it down. However Mickey gradually realised what a great opportunity he was missing and asked to join the TARDIS crew, travelling with the Doctor until he decided to stay to defeat the Cybermen on a parallel Earth.

ADAM

The Doctor met Adam Mitchell on Earth in 2012, and Rose persuaded him to let Adam come with them in the TARDIS. However it soon became clear that Adam wasn't cut out for the time travelling life, and was unceremoniously dumped back home.

CAPTAIN JACK

Con man Captain Jack Harkness travelled with the Doctor until he was killed by the Daleks on the Game Station. Rose brought Jack back to life, but the TARDIS flew off without him. The Doctor decided not to go back for Jack, thinking he would be busy rebuilding the Earth.

TEST YOUR KNOWLEDGE

THE DALEKS

In the ancient legends of the Dalek Homeworld the Doctor is known as the Oncoming Storm — the only person in the universe that the Daleks fear. The Doctor was there for the birth of the Daleks on the planet Skaro and he thought he was there for their destruction at the end of the Time War, but he was wrong. He was distressed when he found a single surviving Dalek in 21st century Utah, believing that his sacrifices in the war had all been in vain. But this was nothing compared to the revelation that a Dalek ship had fallen through time and the fearsome Emperor Dalek had created a new army out of dead humans.

THE CYBERMEN

The people of Earth's twin planet, Mondas, grew weak, so Mondasian scientists began replacing feeble human parts with strong metal ones. Over time, the only piece that was left of each Mondasian was the brain, with all emotions removed. Every other part was cybernetic. These flesh and metal creatures became known as Cybermen and they embarked on universal conquest. It was up to the Doctor to defeat their many plans. The Doctor fought the Cybermen again and again in this universe, but he was shocked to land on a parallel Earth, and find that the monsters were being created there, too. Dying genius John Lumic had found a way to preserve his life and create an army. He told the Doctor that the Cybermen would bring peace but the Doctor knows from experience that they only cause pain and fear.

REPAIR DROIDS

These terrifying clockwork robots have just one purpose — to repair their damaged spaceship. They are programmed to use whatever they can find to make repairs, and to them a human being is just a walking set of spare parts. First the human is knocked out using the hypodermic needle that springs from the droid's hand, then its wrist-blade can be used to dismember the body.

The robots disguised themselves with wigs and masks to infiltrate 18th-century France to find the last part they needed: Madame de Pompadour's brain. But underneath the masks, they have no faces. All that can be seen is the clockwork mechanism that drives them. As long as they are wound up, the droids can go on for ever. Well, unless the Doctor's on the case.

THE SYCORAX

The cruel Sycorax travel through space targeting the planets of weaker species. They employ techniques such as blood control to gain power, but if that fails, they have the full might of the Sycorax Armada behind them. When the Sycorax turned their attention to Earth, thinking it was weak and undefended, it seemed as though they would succeed in their plan to plunder its minerals and take its people into slavery. But they'd reckoned without the Doctor. Even the Sycorax's deadly flesh-searing whips held no fear for the newly regenerated Time Lord, who sent the message to aliens everywhere. The Earth is defended.

TEST YOUR KNOWLEDGE

THE TIME WAR

The Time Lords lived apart from the rest of the universe on their planet of Gallifrey. They observed what was going on elsewhere, but they did not interfere. At least not officially. If there was something that needed to be done, they called on the Doctor to do their dirty work.

But then the threat to the Time Vortex became so great that the Time Lords had to act themselves to save it. The Time War, the most terrible of all Time Wars, was fought between the Time Lords and the evil Daleks. It led to tragedy for both races and for many more caught up in the war.

The Doctor fought alongside his people in the war, and desperately tried to save the many planets that were caught up in the conflict, such as the homeworld of the Nestene Consciousness. He finally ended the war, destroying the Daleks in an inferno. But the Time Lords and their planet burnt at the same time. The Doctor hadn't planned to survive, but he did, the last of his race.

The war took a terrible toll on the Doctor. Having lost his home planet and all his people, he was haunted by the terrible memories of what happened, and his inability to stop it. For the first time in his many lives, he was unsure of himself. But salvation came in the form of Rose Tyler. She helped the Doctor embrace life again, and be happy...

REGENERATION

A Time Lord can live for hundreds of years, but over that length of time his body may wear out and if so, he can decide to change it for another one. This is called regeneration.

It's not always a matter of choice, though. If a Time Lord has a fatal accident the same process allows him to cheat death. Every cell in his body is renewed, and the Time Lord becomes a completely new person. In emergencies like this, the Time Lord has no choice over what new body he gets, and the forced regeneration may go wrong, causing the Doctor to become ill.

The Doctor has regenerated nine times, for many different reasons:

1. Body wearing out.

2. Appearance changed by the Time Lords.

3. Poisoned by radiation.

4. Falling off a radio telescope.

5. Infected with Spectrox Toxaemia.

6. Hitting his head on the TARDIS console.

7. Shot by a street gang.

8. We don't know. Was the Doctor hurt defeating the Daleks in the Time War?

9. Absorbing the energy of the Time Vortex to save Rose.

TEA

When the Doctor absorbed the Time Vortex, he cheated death by regenerating. But what helped him recover from the regeneration itself? The answer is simple — tea!

The drink tea is made from the leaves and berries of the tea plant, which are dried and then brewed with boiling water. Many people then add milk, lemon or sugar to make the tea taste nicer.

Tea fights free radicals, which are dangerous molecules. They occur naturally in the body, but are also produced by pollution. Substances called antioxidants help stop free radicals doing too much damage. Tannin is an antioxidant. It also helps fight bacteria and viruses. Tannin tastes very bitter, and funnily enough a lot of plants contain it to stop animals eating them, but it doesn't stop people drinking tea!

It's not just the Doctor who needs tea to wake him up, lots of humans like to have a cup of tea first thing in the morning as well!

TEST YOUR KNOWLEDGE

THE TARDIS

The TARDIS is not just a spaceship, it's the Doctor's home. The initials TARDIS stand for 'Time and Relative Dimension in Space' and the ship is dimensionally transcendental, which means it's bigger on the inside than the outside. The TARDIS has a chameleon circuit which is supposed to disguise the ship so it fits in with its surroundings, but the circuit got stuck during a visit to the 1960s, and now the TARDIS always looks like a police box. It doesn't fly like a normal spaceship, but dematerialises in one place and appears somewhere else.

By the way, did we mention? It also travels in time.

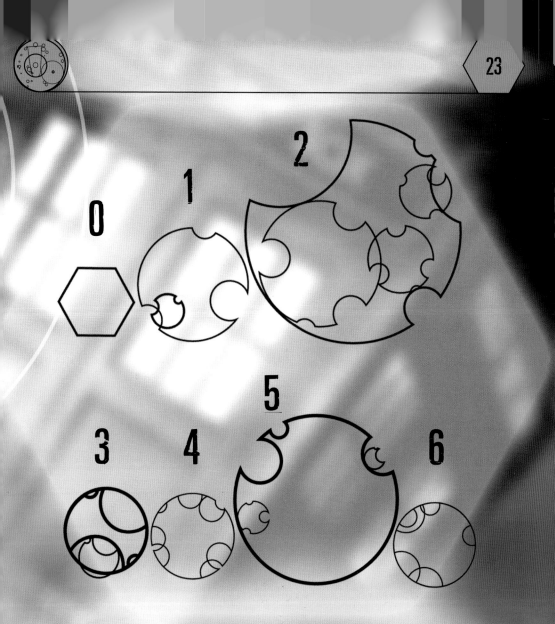

NUMBERS

The Doctor is an expert in maths and science, which allows him to understand advanced technology like the TARDIS. But the TARDIS isn't programmed using Earth numbers — the Doctor uses a Gallifreyan method of counting.

THE SONIC SCREWDRIVER

The Doctor would be in a hole without his sonic screwdriver. This marvellous device can do almost anything, apart from triplicate the flammability of alcohol! It can:

- Reattach barbed wire
- Cut off remote signals
- Reverse teleportation
- Resonate concrete
- Open any lock — except a deadlock seal
- Burn through rope
- Disable security cameras
- Operate the TARDIS by remote control
- And of course, put up cabinets!

PSYCHIC PAPER

If the Doctor needs to get into a restricted area, assume a fake identity or just crash a party, his psychic paper is invaluable. When someone looks at it, they see whatever the Doctor wants them to see. It's come to his rescue on many occasions: from gaining access to the Earthdeath ceremony on Platform One, to persuading people he's working for the management of Satellite Five or has been appointed as protector to Queen Victoria. It even carries messages, such as when the Face of Boe summoned him to New Earth. With psychic paper in his wallet and a sonic screwdriver in his pocket, the Doctor can't be stopped!

TEST YOUR KNOWLEDGE

THE CHRISTMAS INVASION

The TARDIS first brought the new Doctor to Earth, on Christmas Eve, just as the evil Sycorax launched an attack on the planet. But the Doctor, recovering from his recent regeneration, had to wake up before he could try to defeat the aliens!

POLICE TELEPHONE

ATTACK OF THE GRASKE

The alien Graske take over a planet by replacing its population with duplicates. The Doctor discovered a Graske had infiltrated a family Christmas on present-day Earth, and then followed it back to London in 1883. The Graske escaped to its home planet, Griffoth, and the Doctor followed to rescue the humans who'd been replaced.

NEW EARTH

When the Doctor and Rose visited the planet of New Earth, they found their old enemy Cassandra lurking in a hospital basement. But she wasn't responsible for the deadly secret that the cat-like nurses were hiding in the intensive care ward...

TOOTH AND CLAW

In 1879, Her Majesty Queen Victoria, together with the Doctor and Rose, sought shelter in a Scottish manor house. Little realising that they'd been deliberately lured there by werewolves who wanted a lycanthrope on the throne. For their help, the Doctor and Rose were dubbed Sir Doctor of TARDIS and Dame Rose of the Powell Estate.

SCHOOL REUNION

Reports of UFOs from Mickey and a school that got record results brought the Doctor and Rose to present-day Earth, where they had to defeat the evil Krillitanes. But the Doctor's old friend Sarah Jane was also investigating the strange goings-on, and the Doctor discovered what effect he has on the people he leaves behind.

THE GIRL IN THE FIREPLACE

A strange conduit between a spaceship and 18th-century France led to the Doctor's life becoming entwined with that of the beautiful Madame de Pompadour, whom he had to save from terrifying clockwork robots of the future which had been tracking her since childhood.

RISE OF THE CYBERMEN/ THE AGE OF STEEL

The TARDIS fell through the Vortex and landed on a parallel Earth, in time for the Doctor to witness the birth of one of his deadliest enemies. In this universe, John Lumic's Cybus Industries was poised to take over the world — by 'upgrading' every human into an emotionless metal Cyberman.

OTHER ADVENTURES

The Doctor has had many other adventures, such as investigating the disappearance of faces in 1950s England and helping the alien Isolus during the 2012 Olympics. And you can guarantee there are plenty more to come. Wherever there's danger and excitement, you're sure to find the Doctor!

TEST YOUR KNOWLEDGE

ANSWERS

Meet the Doctor
1(b)   2(a)   3(a)   4(c)   5(b)

Companions
1(b)   2(c)   3(b)   4(c)   5(a)

Enemies
1(b)   2(a)   3(b)   4(c)   5(b)

Time Lords
1(a)   2(c)   3(c)   4(b)   5(a)

Technology and Transport
1(a)   2(a)   3(c)   4(a)

Tenth Doctor's Travels
1(b)   2(a)   3(b)   4(c)   5(a)

THE HERO FACTOR

THE HERO FACTOR

"Told you so!" The Doctor drained his cup of tea and turned to Rose on the sunlounger beside him. "If you want the best cuppa in the known universe – and at least half of the unknown universe, for that matter – come to the Warp Hotel on Askenflatt Minor."

"It's a good place to top up your tan, too," Rose agreed, wriggling her bare toes as she gazed about the quiet hotel terrace. "Four suns in the sky and an everlasting summer! I could live here. Let's get a holiday home."

He peered at her over the top of his sunglasses. "You haven't seen Askenflatt Major, yet. The sea's like warm custard and you can ride these funny red dolphin things… Mind you, the tea's not quite as good.

The coffee's actually better, but not the tea. I like the tea here."

Rose sighed happily. "Better stay here a while then, hadn't we?"

"Yup!" the Doctor agreed. "Waiter! Another pot of tea, please, quick as you like…"

Suddenly a gaggle of strange creatures with microphones and TV cameras came rushing up to surround them.

"Blimey, that was quick!" said the Doctor staring round in alarm. "Think you forgot the milk and sugar though. And the tea."

"Leave it out!" Rose recoiled as a

camera was shoved in her face. "Doctor, I think they're reporters!"

"Miss Tyler," said a strange, tusked creature. "Can you tell us what it's like to travel with the future Champion of Askenflatt?"

Rose frowned. "Who's that, then?"

"Why, the Doctor, of course!" roared a skinny red thing, nudging the tusked reporter aside. "The man who will lay down his life to defend the people of Askenflatt from the dreaded Hasval the Destroyer!"

"Lay down my life? I'm lying down on a sunbed! Or rather, I was." The Doctor jumped up crossly and tried to shoo the reporters back a bit. "The dreaded who? What are you lot on about?"

A deep blue alien that was half-man, half-octopus slapped a friendly tentacle about his shoulders. "Come with us, Future Champion of Askenflatt," it said. "*The Solar News Show* is about to begin, and Jazami Paxxo has chosen you to be his special guest!"

"Yeah?" the Doctor brightened a bit. "He's the most famous interviewer in the known universe. And at least half the unknown…"

"Doctor!" cried Rose. A blue glow was enveloping both the Doctor and the octo-man. "What's happening?"

The octo-man gently took her hand with another tentacle. "Just a quick interview, Miss Tyler…" And suddenly the blue glow was sucking her in too. The sunny hotel terrace faded away, and Rose felt herself travelling through space…

Then everything went very, very dark.

The next thing the Doctor knew, a spotlight was shining in his face and loud, dramatic music was playing. "Welcome to *The Solar News Show*," boomed a deep, serious voice. "Tonight, as Hasval the Destroyer advances on the defenceless Askenflatt system, Jazami Paxxo talks to the planets' only hope… the Doctor!"

Suddenly a wave of applause burst out. The light swung away from the Doctor's eyes and he saw he was in a huge TV studio in front of a huge audience, all dressed in black with 4-D view-spex. Six cameras were trained on him like huge guns. And beside him at a sleek news desk sat a tall, grey humanoid with three small ears and an enormous mouth – Jazami Paxxo.

"Welcome, Doctor," growled Paxxo. "Tonight we shall judge if you are worthy of being Askenflatt's champion."

The Doctor was baffled. "Come again?"

"What makes you think you're qualified for the job?"

"I'm qualified for just about everything," the Doctor replied, "only I don't know what you're on about! Where's Rose? We were having a nice little tea break. When did I ever apply to be a champion?"

"Your friend will be joining us shortly," said Paxxo. "Now, you have a reputation for meddling in the affairs of other worlds, correct?"

"Uh-huh," the Doctor agreed. "I could win a medal for meddling."

"You have fought evil aliens and power-mad dictators on countless planets. How much do you charge for your services?"

"What?" The Doctor stared at him in amazement. "I'm not

for hire! If innocent people are in danger, if bullying beings are trying it on… well. Someone's got to sort it, haven't they? Might as well be me." He grinned suddenly. "I'm pretty good at it after all these centuries!"

"I understand you are over 900 years old," said Paxxo. "Aren't you a bit old for saving worlds?"

"I'm in my prime!" The Doctor pulled a banana from his pocket. "And I'm a deadly aim, so don't get cheeky."

"What weapons do you use?" Paxxo demanded.

"I don't, if I can help it."

"You just said you were a deadly aim!"

The Doctor rolled his eyes. "Yeah – with this banana or a kiwi fruit or a satsuma or something!" He started to peel the banana. "Bit of imagination and a soft fruit can always save the day."

Paxxo watched the Doctor stonily. "Hasval's forces are gathering ready to strike. He will use these worlds as a power base from which to conquer a hundred more!"

The Doctor jumped up. "So why are you wasting my time? If the people of Askenflatt need my help, well then – they've got it."

Paxxo smiled. "Thank you, Doctor. That's all I wanted to know."

Suddenly the studio audience vanished, and so did the set. The Doctor realized he was actually in a dark, dank spaceship, lit eerily with a green glow. The TV cameras were no longer cameras – they were robotic cannons. And Jazami Paxxo had disappeared. In his place stood the same blue octopus-creature who had brought him here.

"This is all a wind-up, isn't it?" said the Doctor gravely. "An intergalactic *You've Been Framed*."

The octopus-creature smiled and waggled a small computer in the Doctor's face. "My hologram generator fooled you completely. There were no reporters, no TV show. But the forces of Hasval the Destroyer are real enough. And I should know..." The octo-man reared up over him, baring rows of sharp teeth. "I am Hasval the Destroyer!"

"What d'you want me to do, ask for your autograph?" The

Doctor calmly took a bite of the banana. "Now, what have you done with Rose?"

Hasval scowled. "My troops were in position, ready to conquer Askenflatt. When one of my spies noticed you were here – the unstoppable, indestructible Doctor! Hero of the innocent and thwarter of a thousand invasions! Did you know of my plans? Would you stand against me? I had to find out!"

"You're meant to be a destroyer," the Doctor said coldly. "Wouldn't it have been easier to destroy me?"

"You, the Lord of

41

Time? You, who have survived a thousand wars? You, of whom it is said even the Daleks lived in fear?"

"Me," agreed the Doctor, "who can eat ten sugary doughnuts in a row without even licking my lips."

"I would have waited until you had left Askenflatt, then invaded... but your friend suggested you could live there. I had to act!" Hasval's eyes narrowed. "But having spoken to you, I now know that you are an overrated buffoon. Your friend is scarier than you – and she's locked up!"

Hasval waved a tentacle and a light came on to reveal Rose, trapped behind bars in a cell built into the wall. "Think I prefer the Warp Hotel," she shouted to the Doctor.

"Never mind," he called back, "have half a banana."

"Wow, thanks," said Rose as she caught it.

"Enough clowning, Doctor," rasped Hasval. "It is time you died!"

"You invader types, you think you're so clever," the Doctor retorted. "But I always beat you. And you know why? Because you always slip up…"

With that, the Doctor gave Hasval a hearty shove. The octopoid invader staggered back and slipped on the banana skin Rose had thrown just behind him. With a cry of rage, he landed flat on his back and the Doctor kicked the hologram generator from his grasp.

One of the robotic cannons trundled towards the Doctor and took aim. "Down, Rose!" he yelled, and dived aside. A bolt of power spat from the cannon, missing him by millimetres – and burned a huge hole in the bars of Rose's cell. The Doctor jumped back up and wrestled with the cannon, span it round just as it blasted again so it blew one of the other cannons to pieces.

But by now Hasval had flipped himself back to his feet, trembling with rage, his tentacles tearing the air about him. He grabbed hold of the Doctor, lifted him off his feet and hurled him against the metal floor.

"You pathetic little creature!" Hasval roared, as his robotic cannons advanced on the Doctor. "Did you really think that I, Hasval the Destroyer could be defeated by… a banana?"

"Well…" The Doctor gave a crooked smile. "With a bit of imagination…"

And suddenly, to Hasval's horror, there were two Doctors lying in front of him. A moment later, six of them were getting to their feet. Then twenty. Soon, fifty were standing there, eyes wide and dangerous, smiling at him insolently.

"This is how I am more than a match for pathetic wannabe invaders like you, Hasval!" he bellowed, and suddenly there were well over a hundred Doctors, all speaking as one. "Now, leave this sector of space and renounce your ways of war!"

Hasval gulped. "And… and if I don't?"

The Doctor's eyes flashed – all 250 of them. "You really don't want to know…"

"The stories were right!" wailed Hasval. "You are unstoppable!" With that, he threw open a heavy door and ran from the room, his robotic cannons trundling after him. "Navigator!" he shouted as he ran for his life. "Turn this ship around, we're going home! Disband the fleet! Move it!"

The Doctors watched him go. Then they all threw back their heads and laughed – before vanishing as Rose turned off the hologram projector. Suddenly there was only one Doctor standing in the eerie green room – the Doctor.

"Well, when I turned on the stupid thing I didn't think that would happen!" Rose admitted. "Er… what did happen?"

"Remember the TV audience?" The Doctor tapped his nose. "They all looked identical because Hasval simply took an image of one person and used the hologram generator to duplicate it over and over. The generator must still have been on that setting when you activated it and waved it in my direction."

Rose blushed as she looked down at the generator. "I thought it might be the remote control for those cannon things!"

"That would have worked too," the Doctor mused, smiling as he joined her. "And that's really how I beat my enemies – by choosing my friends very, very carefully!"

Rose grinned and crossed to a computer panel beside the cell. "I know what this is, anyway – it's the teleport that octopus-features used on us."

"Then let's use it to get back to our little holiday," said the Doctor, smacking his lips. "After all this, I bet our tea's gone stone cold. What d'you reckon, shall we push the boat out, get a fresh pot?"

Rose grinned at him as the blue glow took them both back to Askenflatt Minor. "My shout," she said, "for my hero!"

DOCTOR · WHO

OTHER GREAT FILES TO COLLECT